The Star Tree

A Christmas Bedtime Story

Story by Gene G. Bradbury

Illustrated by Victoria Wickell-Stewart

BookWilde Children's Books

ISBN 978-0-9897585-6-7

All inquiries should be addressed to:
BookWilde Children's Books
422 Williamson Rd.
Sequim, WA 98382
www.genegbradbury.com

Printed by CreateSpace, an Amazon.com company.

BookWilde Children's Books

Please visit the author's website:
www.genegbradbury.com

This Adventure is Dedicated to:

My children Deanna, Denise, and Hannah who all love Christmas,
and my sons-in-law Jeff and Craig, who celebrate with them.

Gene G. Bradbury

My granddaughter. May your first Christmas be magical,
followed by many more surrounded by those you love.

Victoria Wickell-Stewart

"It's Christmas Eve and a special night in the forest," said Grandfather.

"Do the forest animals know about Christmas?" asked Jody.

Grandfather looked out the window.
"Yes, the birds are looking toward Star Meadow."

"Mr. and Mrs. Squirrel are making a racket in the trees."

"The deer are on the move, and . . .

Mr. Rabbit is sniffing the wind."

"Where do the animals go on Christmas Eve?" asked Jody.

"All the creatures gather each year
when snow covers the ground and the sky is clear."

"They travel when the moon is like a rocking chair in the night sky and the spider's web glistens in the moonlight."

"The forest creatures go to see the pine tree dressed in stars.
Put on your coat and stocking cap. We'll go see."

By the light of the rocking-chair moon, Grandfather led the way.
Their boots crunched on the newly fallen snow.

Jody heard the birds in the trees.

A deer stared at them from the underbrush.

Jody saw Mr. Rabbit's footprints in the snow.

Darkness covered the forest as they neared the meadow.
Grandfather raised a finger to his lips, "Hush now."

The moon hung ghostly in the night sky.

"But there are no stars," said Jody. And then she saw . . .

the biggest tree she'd ever seen. Its limbs wore white sleeves of snow.
"It's just like the king's robe in my storybook," said Jody.

Grandfather pointed to the animals beneath the tree.
"Be very still," he whispered.

In the meadow all the creatures held their breath when they saw the
first bright star appear below the crescent moon.

Jody looked up into the dark sky. A second star appeared.
Then the night filled with stars. In that moment Jody knew that the
world was a beautiful place in which to live.

All the creatures
turned to the star tree.
Tomorrow, beneath its
branches, they would
sing songs of Christmas.

But tonight the animals would sleep under the most beautiful tree of all.

All except the owl, who stayed awake on Christmas Eve.

Merry Christmas

Good Night!

BookWilde Children's Books

Other Books by the Author

THE MOUSE WITH WHEELS IN HIS HEAD

Meet Fergus who wants to be the first mouse to ride the new Ferris Wheel at the World's Fair. Can a tiny mouse find a way to hitch a ride without being discovered? Follow Fergus's adventure at the 1893 Chicago Exhibition.

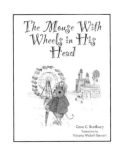

THE MOUSE WHO WANTED TO FLY

Adventure is in Fergus's blood. His success in riding the Ferris Wheel is in the past. When Fergus learns that two brothers, Orville and Wilbur, are going to fly the first powered airplane, Fergus is eager for a new adventure. Is it possible that a mouse can be on the first flight at Kitty Hawk?

FERGUS OF LIGHTHOUSE ISLAND

Fergus, unlike his great uncle, isn't brave at all. He isn't looking for adventure. But when a hurricane threatens Lighthouse Island, adventure finds him. What will Fergus decide when the hurricane threatens the residents of Mouse Village? It's no place for a mouse who is afraid.

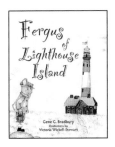

MISCHIEVOUS MAX, A TEDDY BEAR STORY

In Leon's room you will find many teddy bears. Most of them are soft and wonderful to take to bed. But there is one bear who Leon never takes to bed. His name is Max Bear and his fur tickles and his eyes are beastly. Leon knows something else about Max Bear. What if Leon tries sleeping with Max Bear for just one night? Would that be so bad? Leon is about to find out.

The above books are illustrated by Victoria Wickell-Stewart
and are available through the author's website: genegbradbury.com;
and through Amazon.com, Createspace.com, and other retail outlets.

CLOUD CLIMBER

What were his parents thinking, leaving him for three boring weeks at his grandparent's farm? There would be no internet or cable television and what was worse, only Cousin Emily for company. But on a trip to town with his grandfather, Seth learns of Three Friends Hill and the Banshee's Cave. Are these linked to the discovery of a giant kite Seth and Emily find in the old barn? The three weeks literally fly past and the cousins find that Boring Farm is not so boring after all.

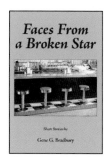

FACES FROM A BROKEN STAR, Short Stories

There was a time when traveling across country one might pull into any small town in America and find a mom and pop cafe. It was a good place to order a fried chicken dinner. Farmers gathered there to compare crop prices and check the weather before working in the field. The local café has disappeared. In these stories you're invited to meet the regulars at the Broken Star Cafe. Some of the characters may sound familiar. Others who will make you laugh and cry.

Poetry Books by Gene G. Bradbury

TRAVELING IN COMPANY

We never travel on our journey alone, but are linked by birth to others. They have walked before us and we follow in their footsteps. Those we come to know best on our travels we call family. From them we learn how to live. Others we meet along the way may lead us to quiet paths of reflection and spiritual practice. In this book of poems the author invites us to look at the many ways we are influenced by others as we travel together.

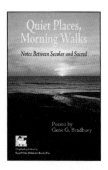

QUIET PLACES, MORNING WALKS:

Notes Between Secular and Sacred

In this book of poetry the author invites the reader to find time each day for quiet and reflection. Each poem is a poetic response to a Psalm verse. The Psalm itself is rewritten in haiku. The book of poetry is prefaced with *morning litanies* to begin the day. The book ends with *evening songs* to end the day. The collection of verse can be used in the morning or evening as a time of quiet and devotion.

SAUNTERING WITH THOREAU

These poems begin with the author's love of Henry David Thoreau's Journals. Each poem is a reflection on a single quote by Thoreau. The poetry is a brief walk with the nineteenth century naturalist through the woods and along the rivers of Concord. Each poem invites the reader to look intently at the things around them and appreciate the place where they live. In Thoreau's words we are invited to find the kernel of life and not just the husk.

All Gene G. Bradbury books are available
through the author's website:
genegbradbury.com;
and through Amazon.com,
Createspace.com, and other retail outlets.